SOCCER TROPHY
MYSTERY

SPORTS STORY

PEACHTREE

ATLANTA

Published by
PEACHTREE PUBLISHING COMPANY INC.
1700 Chattahoochee Avenue
Atlanta, Georgia 30318-2112
www.peachtree-online.com

Text © 2021 by Fred Bowen
Illustrations © 2021 by Marcelo Baez

Edited by Vicky Holifield
Cover design by Kate Gartner
Art Direction by Adela Pons
Composition by Lily Steele

Printed in September 2021 by Lake Book Manufacturing in Melrose Park,
Illinois, in the United States of America

10 9 8 7 6 5 4 3 2 1 (paperback)
First Edition
HC 978-1-68263-078-5
PB 978-1-68263-079-2

Cataloging-in-Publication Data is available from the Library of Congress.

For my wife, Peggy Jackson

There is no way I could have written this book (and all the other books) without her love and support. Thanks again and again.

CHAPTER
ONE

"Go to the middle." Aiden Connelly quickly tapped the soccer ball from his right foot to his left foot and sprinted toward the middle of the field.

Down a goal, he thought. *We've got to score...fast.*

Aiden slipped a pass to Daniel Novak, his friend and Thunder teammate, who was charging down the right wing. Daniel tried to swing a crossing pass toward the front of the goal. The ball sailed wide and over the goal line. The referee signaled that it was the Avengers ball.

"Get back!" Coach Schmidt called out, waving his hands on the sidelines.

Aiden hustled back, thinking about the

game situation with every step. *Down 2–1. Just a few minutes to play. If we can't beat the Avengers, we really need to salvage a point in the county league standings with a tie.*

Aiden stepped in front of an Avenger forward to regain possession of the ball. He raced up the field, checking the defense. All the Avengers were dropping back, clogging the passing lanes.

Aiden and his teammates swung the ball from side to side, looking for an opening. Jayden Jefferson, a Thunder midfielder, sent a long, high ball in toward the goal. Thunder and Avenger players scrambled to get a head or a leg on the ball.

The ball spun loose from the tangle of players. Daniel kicked it hard with his left foot, spinning it through the air toward the net.

Just before it reached the goal, the ball smacked against the arm of an Avenger defender.

"Hands!" Aiden screamed along with his Thunder teammates.

Tweeeeeeet!

The referee blew her whistle and pointed

to the penalty mark twelve yards in front of the goal.

The Thunder had a penalty kick!

Coach Schmidt stepped out onto the field. "Have Jayden take it!" he shouted. "Pick out a side and let it go. Just like in practice."

Jayden set down the ball on the penalty mark. Aiden lined up with Daniel along the line in back of the penalty mark, ready to burst in if the goalkeeper made a save and the ball was loose.

The Avengers goalkeeper bounced from side to side along the goal line, trying to guess where Jayden would kick the ball. He dove to the right as Jayden made contact with the ball, but he'd guessed wrong. Jayden blasted the ball to the left.

Goal! The game was tied, 2–2.

The ball stayed in the middle of the field for the remaining minutes with neither team generating a single shot on goal. Finally the referee blew her whistle and crossed her hands over her head to signal the end of the game.

"We were *so* lucky to squeak by like that," Aiden said to Daniel as the teammates walked slowly from the pitch. "We should have beat those guys easy."

Daniel reached into his gym bag and pulled out his phone. His fingers moved swiftly across the screen, and the standings for the twelve-team Winchester County U-14 soccer league appeared.

TEAM	W-L-T	POINTS
Fury	7-0-2	23
Thunder	7-1-1	22
Wolfpack	6-2-1	19
Gunners	6-3-0	18
Dragons	5-2-2	17
Tigers	5-4-0	15
Red Bulls	4-5-0	12
Avengers	3-5-1	10
Lemonheads	3-6-0	9
Vipers	3-6-0	9
United Blue	1-8-0	3
Wolverines	0-8-1	1

"They've already posted the results of all of today's games," Daniel said. "Man, they are fast."

The boys studied the top part of the league standings. "The tie means we're now one point behind the Fury," Aiden said.

"Yeah, we'd better beat the Wolfpack and the Dragons in our last two games if we want to get on the trophy." Daniel tossed the phone into his bag. "And hope somebody beats or ties the Fury."

"We can do it," Aiden said, even though he wasn't 100 percent sure they could.

"Good game!" Aiden's father called out as he walked across the field toward them.

"We were lucky," Aiden said. "Hey, Dad. What—?"

"Two twenty," his dad said, reading Aiden's mind. "We've still got time to catch the end of Ava's game."

Aiden, his father, and Daniel walked quickly past several soccer fields at the Taylor Park Soccerplex. As they approached the field where his twin sister Ava's team was playing, Aiden saw his mother standing on the sidelines.

"Spread out!" she yelled through cupped hands. "Move the ball! Come on, hustle!"

"What's the score?" Aiden asked her.

"Two to nothing," she answered without taking her eyes off the field.

"How's Ava doing?"

"Not bad. She's scored both goals."

Aiden's gaze locked on his sister. He shook his head, marveling at how easily Ava controlled play—distributing the ball, directing her teammates. Always in control, never in a hurry, head up, probing the defense for a weakness.

Sensing an opening, Ava darted forward and slipped by a defender. As another defender stepped forward to challenge, Ava skidded a perfect pass to a closing wing, who then directed a shot toward the far post past the diving goalkeeper. The ball hit the inside of the post and spun into the net.

Goal!

Aiden's mom jumped up. "Great pass, Ava! Way to keep your head up."

Aiden threw his hands into the air in disbelief. "Did you see that pass?"

Daniel nodded. "That was sweet. Your sister's got magic in her feet."

A few minutes later, Ava and her Spirit teammates celebrated their 3–0 victory by thrusting their index fingers toward the sky.

"They're awfully happy for such an easy win," Daniel said.

Aiden's mother smiled. "They're excited because they won their league."

"Already?"

"Yeah," Aiden said. "They have two more games, but no one can catch them now."

Daniel took out his phone and checked the U-14 girls' standings. "I see what you mean," he said. "They're way ahead."

When Ava came off the field, her face was red and streaming with sweat. She was smiling from ear to ear.

"You won!" Aiden shouted as their mom and dad wrapped her up in a big hug.

"We're on the trophy," Ava said with a satisfied smile. "We're on the trophy."

CHAPTER
TWO

Aiden, Ava, and Daniel bolted up the county library steps, taking them two at a time.

"What's the big rush?" Daniel asked. "The books aren't going anywhere."

"We want to make sure we each get a copy," Ava said.

Aiden agreed. "Since Ms. Sanchez assigned the book to our Advanced English class yesterday, everybody will be trying to get a copy of the book."

"Yeah, right," Daniel sighed as they pushed open the door and entered the library. "The big reward for getting into Advanced English is that we get to read boring stuff like *The Age of*...whatever it's called."

"*The Age of Innocence* by Edith Wharton," Ava said. "Okay, Daniel. What exciting books did you read over the summer?"

"*Backfield Boys* by John Feinstein," he said. "It's a sports mystery."

"I've read his books," Aiden said. "They're cool. But there's no way Ms. Sanchez is going to assign a mystery for Advanced English."

"It won't kill you two to read a classic once in a while," Ava said. "Mom said Edith Wharton was the first woman to win the Pulitzer Prize for literature."

"Big deal. I still don't want to read it," Daniel said.

"Why?" Ava asked. "Because a woman wrote it?"

"No, because I just don't want to read it."

The three friends stopped talking as they stepped into the main reading room. The library was another world, cool and quiet. The only sound was the low murmur of voices at the front desk. Several people sat in high-back chairs in a large, sun-drenched room, reading the newspapers.

"Where do we start?" Aiden asked.

"Ms. Sanchez said there's a special section for the books that are assigned in English classes," Ava said. "We need to ask one of the librarians."

"Hey," Daniel said, pointing to a tall wooden glass case across the room. "Let's go check out the soccer trophies first."

They walked over and stood before the case. Behind the glass stood several shelves of sports trophies representing teams that had won championships over the years. Aiden pulled Daniel and Ava to the corner where the two soccer trophies were displayed. They each had gold soccer players on top and large gold plates on the four sides of the wooden base. Engraved on the plates were the names of all the winning teams for the U-14 county soccer championships, going back many years.

Daniel elbowed Ava. "Your team is going to be next on the list," he said, pointing to the girls' trophy.

"You guys still have a chance," Ava said.

"We've got to beat the Wolfpack and the

Dragons in our last two games," Aiden said. "That's going to be tough."

"I know," Daniel agreed. "They're both good teams."

"But it would be so cool if we could do it," Aiden said, staring at the boys' trophy and picturing the *Thunder* engraved on the list of winning teams.

"Can I help you find anything?" asked Mrs. Salvadore, an older woman with short gray hair and a friendly face. Ava and Aiden had known the librarian since they'd started coming to the library when they were little.

"We're looking for the books on reserve for class assignments. *The Age of Innocence* by Edith Wharton," Ava said. "It's for our Advanced English class."

"I know," Mrs. Salvadore said. "Ms. Sanchez told me all about it. So we should have enough copies."

"Ava's team is going to be on the trophy for this year," Aiden chimed in, pointing to the girls' trophy.

"Wonderful! Congratulations, Ava."

"We still have a chance to get on the boys' trophy," Daniel said.

"You do know that's not the original trophy, don't you?" Mrs. Salvadore asked, keeping her voice soft.

"Really?" Aiden asked.

"The soccer league started about fifty years ago," Mrs. Salvadore explained, lowering her voice even more, "because some parents thought Little League baseball had become too competitive."

"Too competitive?" Daniel asked in a surprised voice. "Soccer is super competitive."

"Yeah, the parents yell on the sidelines nonstop," Ava said. "Soccer games can be pretty intense."

"Well, maybe they thought back then that soccer would be less competitive than baseball. But the original trophy disappeared from the library about forty years ago," Mrs. Salvadore explained.

"Disappeared?" Aiden said in disbelief. "How can something just disappear from a library?"

"Nobody could figure it out. The police

were called in," Mrs. Salvadore continued. "They investigated. It was all in the newspaper, the *Reporter*. I had just started working here. In fact, I worked with your grandmother for several years." She looked over at Ava. "How is she doing, by the way?"

"She's okay," Ava said. "She's 84. She lives over at the Devereaux House nursing home. Sometimes she forgets stuff, but she seems pretty happy. She has lots of friends there."

"Well, be sure to tell her Maria Salvadore says hello," she said and then went back to the story about the missing trophy. "Anyway, the police talked to everyone who worked or volunteered at the library and almost everyone who came in regularly. They never did find the trophy or figure out who took it."

"Is that all that was missing?" Daniel asked.

"As far as I know," the librarian said.

"Why would anyone steal a soccer trophy?" Aiden asked, shaking his head. "It doesn't make sense."

"That's what the police kept saying," Mrs. Salvadore agreed. "Who would steal a soccer trophy?"

She shrugged. "Anyway, they never figured it out." She turned and motioned for the children to come with her. "I don't think we'll solve the mystery of the missing soccer trophy today, so why don't I get you your copies of *The Age of Innocence*."

Moments later the librarian handed Aiden, Ava, and Daniel each a paperback book. They checked out the books, stepped into the sunlight, and walked slowly down the library steps.

But they were still thinking about the missing soccer trophy.

CHAPTER
THREE

"That was a cool story Mrs. Salvadore told about the soccer trophy," Aiden said.

"Yeah," Daniel said. "I wonder who took it. I mean, it couldn't just disappear."

"Mrs. Salvadore said it happened around forty years ago," Ava said. "There's no way anyone is ever going to figure that one out. Seriously, who would take a kids' soccer trophy?"

"Maybe someone on a team that didn't win it," Aiden suggested.

Daniel frowned at his friend. "I'm not so sure about that," he said. "I mean, I want us to get the Thunder on the trophy as bad as anyone, but I'd never steal the trophy if we didn't win. It wouldn't be worth it. I mean it's not like it's made of gold."

"So you *would* steal the trophy if you thought it was worth it?" Ava teased.

"Come on," Daniel said. "You know what I mean."

"Yeah," said Ava. "We'd better keep an eye on you. You'll steal stuff...if you think it's worth it."

The three friends headed home, following their usual route past Jalal's Barber Shop, Lena's Pizza Parlor, the Book Nook, and Wilson's Drug Store. The late afternoon sun slanted through the big trees along the side of the road.

Aiden was still tossing around the soccer trophy mystery in his head. "Wouldn't it be great if we found the trophy?"

"Didn't you hear what I just said? There's no way. It would be impossible." Ava shook her head. "It's not like we can go out and investigate something that happened way before we were born."

"We'll figure it out the way detectives do

in mysteries. You know, gathering clue
by going around and talking to people who
might know something about the crime."
Aiden's voice got higher and louder as he
talked. "Remember that old show about cold
cases? They'd dig back into the past for new
evidence. Then they'd put it all together...
like the pieces of a puzzle."

"Yeah, in the last part of the episode,"
Daniel added.

"Right," Aiden said, getting really worked
up now. "Exactly like that."

"You guys are crazy," Ava said. "We're
not detectives. And where would we even
start? The trophy was stolen forty years
ago."

They walked in silence for a few steps.

"Don't forget," Daniel said, sounding
more doubtful, "even the police couldn't figure it out the first time. Mrs. Salvadore said
they talked to—"

"Maybe they overlooked something,"
Aiden interrupted. "Or they talked to the
wrong people. Or the people they talked to
lied."

"That's right. You know how it is on TV and in mysteries," Daniel said, now sounding almost as excited as Aiden. "The detective always figures out the case when the police can't."

"This isn't TV!" Ava shouted. "It's Winchester."

"And they always get in a cool car chase," Daniel added.

"You guys can't be serious about this," Ava said, shaking her head. "We're thirteen years old—"

"Almost fourteen," Aiden corrected. "In two months."

"Well, we're definitely not going to get in a car chase," Ava said.

"All right," Aiden said. "Maybe a bike chase." He and Daniel laughed.

But Ava didn't even smile. "Look, I know you guys like mysteries," she said in a calm voice. "But get real. Who is going to talk to us? Even if they could remember any information about something that happened forty years ago."

"We could say we're working on a school

project," Aiden suggested.

"Yeah, a local history project," Daniel added.

"You know how people love to help kids with their school projects," Aiden said.

"My dad loves working on my science projects," Daniel said. "He hardly lets me touch them."

"You're lucky. Maybe he can help Ava and me with our projects." Aiden laughed. "Our parents are always saying we have to do them ourselves."

Aiden turned to his twin sister. "Come on," he pleaded. "It might be fun. We can all work on solving the mystery together. We'd have time after school on the days we don't have soccer practice."

Ava took a deep breath. "All right," she said finally. "I guess I'm in. I'll help out. But I don't think there's any way a bunch of kids are going to figure out a forty-year-old mystery."

"You changed your mind all of a sudden," Daniel said. "What gives? Why do you want to help us now?"

"Because...," Ava said, holding up her paperback book, "I skimmed the first few pages and I can already tell that working on a forty-year-old mystery has got to be more fun than reading *The Age of Innocence*."

CHAPTER
FOUR

P lease get glasses of water for everyone," Aiden and Ava's mother called to them from the kitchen that evening.

"What are we having?" Ava asked as she walked in and looked at the stove.

"Curried chicken with vegetables over rice." Their father began to ladle the steaming food onto plates.

"Smells good," said Ava. "Is it something new?"

"It's new for me," Dad said. "It's your grandmother's recipe."

The family took their plates into the dining room and sat down around the table.

Aiden started to take a bite.

"Watch out, it's hot," Mom warned. "While

you're letting it cool, would you run and get the rolls? They're on the kitchen counter."

Finally, when everyone was ready to eat, Mom started in with her usual questions about school.

"Did you get your copies of *The Age of Innocence* today?"

"Yeah, they had plenty," Ava answered. "No worries."

"We were talking to—" Aiden began.

Before he could finish, Dad interrupted. "*The Age of Innocence*? I didn't read that until high school."

"Remember, Michael, they're in Advanced English," Mom said with a smile, turning back to Ava. "How much time do you have to finish it?"

"We'll read the book as a class. Ms. Sanchez will assign us a certain number of pages each night," Ava explained. "Then we'll discuss the assigned reading the next day."

"Make sure you don't fall behind," Mom warned. "It's hard to catch up when you leave things to the last minute."

"We won't," Aiden assured her and tried

to steer the conversation back to what he wanted to discuss. "We saw Mrs. Salvadore at the library today and she—"

"Do you have much homework tonight?" Mom asked.

"Come on, you guys. How about you let me finish a sentence?"

"Oh, sorry, Aiden. Go ahead."

Aiden glanced over at Ava, who was trying not to laugh. "We saw Mrs. Salvadore at the library and she told us about this mystery—"

"What kind of mystery?" Dad asked. "You mean a book?"

Aiden shook his head. "No, I'm talking about a *real* mystery. The mystery of the disappearing soccer trophy."

"Yeah, it went missing about forty years ago," Ava joined in. "And they never found it."

"That was a long time ago," Mom said as she reached for a roll. "What did Mrs. Salvadore say about it?"

"Not much," Aiden said. "We were wondering if we could figure out who stole it."

"How would you do that?" Mom asked. "I

doubt anyone will remember anything about it now. And anyway, I don't want you doing anything that takes time from your schoolwork."

"We just thought it would be fun to try," Ava said.

"Lisa, maybe they could write an article for the *Reporter*," Dad suggested, looking across the table at his wife. "I'm sure most people in town don't know anything about the trophy going missing."

"That's a better idea," Mom said. "Or maybe write a piece for the school newspaper. But it would be interesting to go more into the history of sports in the town. Not just the missing trophy." She looked back and forth at the twins. "It would be good for you two to get into an activity that isn't just sports—like the school newspaper."

Aiden struggled not to roll his eyes. Their parents were always thinking up projects for him and Ava to work on. Writing an article for the school newspaper didn't sound like as much fun as being a detective and solving a mystery.

"Wasn't your mother working at the library around that time?" Dad asked Mom. "Maybe Aiden and Ava could talk to her about it."

Mom brightened. "That's a great idea. I'm sure Nana would love to have them come by." She looked over at the twins. "But don't bother her with a lot of questions. You know how confused she can get sometimes."

"Do you two have soccer practice tomorrow?" Dad asked.

"I don't."

"Neither do I."

"All right," Mom said. "I'll call the Devereaux House after dinner and tell them to expect you tomorrow after school. But be sure to leave enough time to do your reading and homework."

Mom glanced across the table at Dad and smiled. "Michael, remember back in high school when you and Chris Kopp and Nick Geer used to always hang out at the library?"

Aiden caught Ava's eye. Their parents were always remembering the "old days" like this. They had both grown up in the town. They'd gone to Winchester High School together and were high school sweethearts. It seemed like they'd known each other their whole lives.

Dad laughed. "Yeah. We were supposed to be studying, but I don't remember much studying getting done. Chris and Nick spent most of their time reading the sports magazines while I was always checking out the new sci-fi titles."

"Did you hang out at the library too?" Ava asked her mother.

"Not much. I was usually busy after school."

"Your mother was a big sports star, like you two," Dad said, waving his fork toward the twins. "Soccer, basketball, field hockey. Your mom was the best at all of them."

"They didn't make a big deal out of girls' sports back then," Mom said. "Hardly anyone came to our games."

"*I* did," Dad protested.

"That's just because you wanted to see *me*."

Aiden and Ava traded glances again.

They had heard most of these old stories before.

"And your father," Mom said, "was always the lead in the school plays and musicals."

Dad looked a little embarrassed. "Not *always*."

Mom seemed a bit surprised. "Well, most of the time." And then she added, "And he was always the most handsome young man on the stage."

"Better looking than Chris Kopp?" Dad asked with a sly smile.

"I thought so."

Aiden looked at Ava and sighed. Their parents' high school memories—the days when Mom was teenage Lisa Romano and Dad was a young Michael Connelly—could go on for a while.

Aiden tapped his fingers on the dining room table and hardly listened. All this talk of the old days almost made him wish he was doing his homework—or even reading *The Age of Innocence*.

CHAPTER FIVE

The next day, Aiden and Daniel met at a field in back of a local elementary school for their own version of soccer practice. Aiden let go a strong, right-legged kick that spun the soccer ball high through the air. Standing in front of a battered silver soccer goal frame, Daniel caught the ball with both hands.

"That was a good one!" he shouted. "Nice and high and right in front of the net. I can see Jayden or me heading one like that into the goal."

Aiden checked his phone for the time. "I'd better get going," he said. "I'm supposed to meet Ava at the Devereaux House in ten minutes. We're going to talk to my grandmother about the missing soccer trophy."

"Want me to come?" Daniel asked.

Aiden shook his head. "It's a nursing home. They don't like lots of kids coming in. Just family."

Daniel tucked the ball under his arm. "Maybe I'll go home and Google stolen soccer trophies and see what I can find."

Minutes later, Aiden and Ava walked into the Devereaux House. The lobby was a bright, circular room that looked like it could be in a hotel or a country club.

"We're here to see our grandmother, Mrs. Romano," Aiden told the man at the desk.

The man smiled at their grandmother's name. "Oh, you must be Ava and Aiden. Mrs. Romano is in the sitting room. I believe she's expecting you."

He pointed down the hall. "It's the second door on the right."

Aiden and Ava walked down the hall and stepped into the room. Their grandmother was sleeping in a leather chair. A book was open on her lap. Another woman sat at a

table in the corner of the room doing a jig-
saw puzzle.

Ava walked up to her grandmother and
whispered, "Nana...Nana. Aiden and I came
to see you."

Their grandmother's eyes flickered open.
She smiled when she saw a familiar face.
"Ava," she said softly. "You look so much
like your mother."

Nana sat up in the chair and placed her
book on a wooden side table. "And Aiden,
you'll soon be taller than your father!"

"Mrs. Chang," she said to the woman
working on the puzzle. "These are my grand-
children, Ava and Aiden. They're twins."

Mrs. Chang smiled and nodded and went
back to her puzzle.

Just like their mother always did, Nana
started in with questions about the twins'
schoolwork and sports. "So what books are
you reading? You should always be reading
a book. Reading is very important."

"We have to read *The Age of Innocence* for
school," Ava answered. "We're in Advanced
English this year."

This information seemed to please their grandmother. "Edith Wharton was the first woman to win the Pulitzer Prize for literature, you know," she said.

"We know, Mom told us," Ava said.

"Oh, I loved that book. I don't remember the details now, but I can still picture those fancy houses in New York City and the women in their elegant clothes." Nana put her head back against the chair and smiled.

Aiden was afraid she would fall asleep again, so he got right down to the business that had brought them to the Devereaux House.

"Nana, Ava and I wanted to ask you some questions."

"Is this for a school project? Your mother mentioned something to me about a school assignment."

"Sort of."

"Well, go ahead. What are your questions? I'll try to answer them."

She turned toward the corner of the room. "We're not bothering you are we, Mrs. Chang?"

Mrs. Chang didn't look up from her puzzle.

"She doesn't hear very well," Nana whispered as if she was letting Aiden and Ava in on a secret.

"You used to work at the county library, didn't you, Nana?" Aiden asked.

"Oh yes, many years ago, when your mother and Uncle Tom were young."

"Do you remember," Ava asked, "that a soccer trophy was stolen?"

Their grandmother gave them a confused look. "Someone stole one of your soccer trophies?" she asked.

Aiden jumped in. "No, Nana, no one stole one of *our* trophies." He talked slowly so she could follow. "We want to know if you remember when a county soccer trophy was stolen from the library. Mom said it happened when you were working there."

Nana put her fingers to her lips. Her face had a faraway look as if she was thinking of the past. "Oh, I do remember something about that."

"Can you tell us what happened?" Aiden asked.

"Oh my, yes. It caused a lot of excitement! Nothing had ever gone missing from the library before, except a few books now and then, of course. Once someone came back to the library to return about a dozen books that he had checked out years earlier. I was..."

Aiden could feel his grandmother wandering off the subject so he gently tried to pull her back.

"But someone did take the trophy?" he asked.

"It was a long time ago, you know," she sighed. "I worked at the library to make some extra money when the children were young." She paused, thinking.

"Everything is so expensive these days. I don't know how young people do it. I used to get books out of the library for your grandfather. He loved mysteries. He would stay up all night reading, if it was a good one."

Aiden tried again to guide his grandmother back to the stolen soccer trophy.

"Did the police come and ask questions?"

"About what?"

"The soccer trophy. The one that was stolen out of the library."

"Why, of course the police came. I remember that police detective who asked a lot of questions." She straightened up in her chair. "He even questioned me. You know, I think he thought *I* took the trophy. Can you believe that? Why would I want to take an old trophy? I never stole anything in my life."

"Why did he think you took it, Nana?" Ava asked.

Nana's answer was another tangle.

"Because I used to work late some nights. Your grandfather would take care of the children...your mother and your Uncle Tom. He would let them stay up until all hours."

She shook her finger as if she was scolding someone. "I told him that children need their sleep. For school...for sports. Your mother was a wonderful athlete. Soccer, basketball.... She would have played football if we had let her. She played field hockey in college, you know."

She smiled, still visibly proud of her daughter. Then her face turned cloudy.

"Of course, they didn't make a big deal out of girls' sports back then. It's so different now. They make a big deal out of everything. Too big a deal sometimes, if you ask me."

She shook her head. "Where was I?" she asked.

"Why did the detective think you took the trophy?" Aiden asked.

"Oh yes. Well, I worked late some nights and had to lock up the library after everyone had left. Sometimes I had to push Mr. Bannister out the door. He was always the last to leave. I suppose I had been working late the night before someone noticed the trophy was gone."

Nana looked across the room. "But they never knew exactly when the trophy was taken."

"Do you remember the detective's name?" Ava asked gently.

"Oh goodness, I don't know," she said with a wave of her hand. "It was so long ago. It was probably in the newspaper. A mystery like that was big news in a small town."

She smiled. "Winchester is such a nice town. Your grandfather and I always loved it here. Such a wonderful place to bring up children...everyone is so pleasant...the schools are good and..."

Suddenly Nana seemed tired, as if all the memories were too much. Aiden looked at Ava and nodded. They talked with her a little longer about other things and then got up to leave.

"We'd better get going, Nana."

Minutes later, Aiden and Ava stepped outside into the late afternoon chill.

"I'm not sure that helped us very much," Ava said.

"Well, we did find out a few things," Aiden said. "We know that Nana had a key to the library, although probably lots of people had keys. We know that a detective investigated the theft. And Nana thinks it appeared in the newspaper."

Aiden's phone pinged with a text message

from Daniel. Aiden showed the screen to Ava.

> **BIG news about the soccer trophy mystery!!!!**
> C u tomorrow @ school

"I wonder what that's all about?" Aiden said.

"Text him back and ask him."

Aiden typed in a few words and waited. "No answer," he said. "I guess we'll have to find out tomorrow."

CHAPTER
SIX

Daniel slid into a chair at a lunch table with Aiden and Ava.

"So what's the big news about the soccer trophy mystery?" Aiden asked.

Daniel smiled as if he was pleased with himself. "I went online yesterday to see if there were any articles about—"

"It was forty years ago," Ava interrupted. "They didn't have the internet back then. So you're probably not going to find anything about a soccer trophy that went missing decades ago in a small town."

Daniel continued as if he hadn't heard a word Ava had said.

"So I plugged in 'missing soccer trophy.' I didn't find anything about the Winchester case, but I discovered there's another mystery about a missing soccer trophy." He sat back and folded his arms across his chest.

"What are you talking about?" Aiden asked.

"The World Cup."

"The World Cup?" Aiden blurted out. "You're crazy. The World Cup isn't missing. It's the most famous trophy in the world."

"Yeah," Ava agreed. "They have the trophy at every World Cup. I've seen it on TV."

Daniel leaned forward and pointed his finger at his friends. "I know. But *that* is not the original World Cup."

"What?" Aiden asked.

"Wait," Ava said. "If that's not the real—"

Daniel held up his hands. "Let me tell you the story."

Ava and Aiden scooted their cafeteria chairs closer to Daniel. "So tell us," Aiden said.

"Okay, the World Cup started in 1930 in Uruguay—"

"Where?" Aiden asked.

"You know, Uruguay. In South America." Daniel went on with his story. "Back then they had a gold-plated trophy called 'Victory.' It was named after Nike, the Greek goddess of victory."

"You mean like the shoes?" Ava asked.

"Yeah. Like the shoes." Daniel looked at the twins. "Are you going to let me tell the story?"

"Sorry," said Ava. "Go ahead."

"Anyway, they renamed the trophy after the guy who started the World Cup...some dude named Jules Rimet."

"Doesn't the country that wins the World Cup get to keep the trophy?" Aiden asked. "Until the next tournament?"

"You're right," Daniel said. "Italy won in 1938, but they didn't have the World Cup games in 1942 or 1946 because of World War II. At some point an Italian soccer official took the trophy from a bank where they were keeping it and hid it under his bed so the Nazis wouldn't steal it."

"Is that when it disappeared?" Aiden asked.

"Nope," Daniel said, shaking his head. "The official returned it after the war. But there's more. When England hosted the World Cup in 1966, they displayed the trophy at some fancy hall."

"So?"

"So someone broke in and stole the World Cup."

"And that's when it disappeared?" Aiden asked.

"Would you let me finish? I'm getting to that—"

"Well, you'd better hurry up," Ava protested. "Our lunch period is only forty-five minutes long, you know."

"It'll take forty-five hours if you keep interrupting!" Daniel almost shouted. "I'll try to make it short. The trophy was recovered seven days later when a dog named Pickles found it wrapped up in newspapers in someone's bushes in London."

"Pickles?" Ava said. "That's a dumb name for a dog."

"So what if it's a dumb name for a dog?" Daniel said, clearly getting impatient.

"So they got the trophy back," Aiden said. "I thought you said it disappeared."

Daniel gave Aiden and Ava a warning look. "So...in 1970 Brazil won the World Cup for a third time. And under the rules they got to keep the trophy...permanently."

"That's when Pelé played for Brazil," Aiden said. "So now Brazil has the original trophy?"

"They did for a while," Daniel explained. "They put it on display at the Brazilian Football Confederation headquarters behind bulletproof glass and everything."

"But somebody took it?" Aiden asked.

"You got it," Daniel said, pointing at Aiden. "Back in 1983, somebody broke into the display case and stole the trophy."

"Did they ever find out who took it?" Aiden asked.

"The Brazilian police convicted four guys for the crime," Daniel said. "But they never found the trophy."

"Wait," Ava said. "So what's the trophy they hold up at the World Cup today?"

"It's a replacement."

"And they never found the original trophy?" Aiden said.

"Nope," Daniel said, leaning back in his chair. "It's a mystery. Just like what happened to our county's soccer trophy."

"I'm not sure the World Cup mystery helps us solve *our* mystery," Ava said.

"Maybe we should find a dog named Pickles," Aiden said with a laugh. "To help us find our trophy."

Daniel sighed. "Well, what did you find out from your grandmother?" he asked as he went back to eating his lunch.

Aiden and Ava traded glances. "Not much," Aiden said. "The police investigated, but Nana couldn't remember the officer's name. She said it was big news in town and was in the newspaper. But no one ever figured out who did it or what happened to the trophy."

"Maybe we can find the newspaper articles," Daniel said. "They might give us a clue...like the name of the police officer, for instance."

"Where are we going to find them?" Ava

asked. "I don't think a little newspaper like the *Reporter* has its old editions on the internet."

"Maybe they're at the newspaper office," Aiden said. "Or at the library. They've got lots of old stuff. I think we should at least go look."

"You know what I think?" Daniel said, looking at Aiden.

"What?"

"I think we'd better beat the Wolfpack on Saturday or we'll never get our team name on any soccer trophy."

CHAPTER
SEVEN

Daniel ran to the edge of the soccer field where Aiden was waiting.

"Did you hear the big news?"

"What news?" Aiden asked.

"The Red Bulls tied the Fury, 1–1."

"Seriously?"

"Seriously," Daniel said. "That means if we win today and earn three more points, we'll be one point ahead of them going into the last week of the season."

Daniel pulled up the league standings on his phone and studied the top teams.

TEAM	W-L-T	POINTS
Fury	7-0-3	24
Thunder	7-1-1	22
Gunners	7-3-0	21
Dragons	6-2-2	20
Wolfpack	6-2-1	19

Aiden looked down the columns, then said, "We've still got to beat the Wolfpack today. If they win their last two games, they'll have an outside shot at first place too."

"No worries," Daniel said with a wave of his hand. "We'll beat them."

Aiden wished he could be as confident—or overconfident—as Daniel. He looked across the pitch to the Wolfpack players, who were warming up.

They aren't going to be pushovers, he thought.

Aiden was right. The Wolfpack came out hustling and playing hard. The Thunder seemed to be one step behind the Wolfpack the whole first half. Only a couple of diving saves by Alex Ricci, the Thunder goalkeeper, kept the score knotted at 0–0 at the half.

Aiden and Daniel sat on the grass during halftime sucking on orange slices and listening to Coach Schmidt, who paced in front of the team.

"We've got to step it up, guys," he said. "We need a win here. Let's be more aggressive. Take a few chances." Coach looked straight at Aiden and Daniel. "You guys have to attack more. Put some pressure on their keeper. He hardly touched the ball in the first half."

As Aiden turned to go back onto the field, his mother called him over to the touchline.

"Take the ball up the sidelines more." She motioned with her hand. "Spread the defense out and then look for Daniel or Jayden in the middle."

Aiden nodded. When it came to soccer, or really any sport, his mom knew what she was talking about. He hustled back onto the field.

"Be aggressive!" his mom shouted.

The opening minutes of the second half brought more of the same pattern as in the first half. The Wolfpack dominated play and continued to put pressure on the Thunder goalkeeper. The minutes piled up with the ball staying in the Thunder end. It seemed like only a matter of time before the Wolfpack scored.

When a Wolfpack wing lifted a dangerous crossing pass toward the Thunder goal, Alex jumped out and snagged the ball out of the air. Then with one quick step he passed the ball down the sideline toward Aiden.

It only took one touch for Aiden to bring the bouncing ball under control and race up the sideline. He crossed midfield and, remembering his mother's advice, looked for his teammates in the middle of the field.

Aiden slipped by a Wolfpack defender with a crossover touch and spied Daniel streaking up the center of the field. He sent a low ball skimming along the grass to the top of the penalty area.

Two of the Wolfpack defenders converged

to cover Daniel. Without wasting a second, Daniel timed his kick, meeting the ball while still on the run.

The shot glanced off a defender and angled just wide, bouncing across the end line.

"Corner kick!" The referee pointed to the right edge of the field.

Aiden raced over and set up the ball on the chalk line near the red corner flag. He raised his right hand, stepped forward, and sent the ball spinning high and hard toward the front of the goal, just like in his practice sessions with Daniel.

The Wolfpack goalkeeper stepped out to grab the ball but got tangled up with the mass of crashing bodies near the goal. The ball bounced free. With a quick touch, Jayden gathered it in and took a swipe at the ball with his left foot.

Thunk!

Jayden's foot caught the ball flush, sending it right for the Wolfpack goal. His view still blocked by the bodies in front of the net, the Wolfpack goalkeeper didn't have a chance. The ball flew straight and true. The net jumped back.

Goal! The Thunder led 1–0.

While the team celebrated, Coach Schmidt paced along the sidelines, yelling and waving his arms. "Back on defense! Forwards and midfielders help out. Everybody hustle!"

"How much time is left?" Aiden asked as he jogged back to the Thunder half of the field.

Coach checked his watch. "About five minutes. But don't worry about the time. Get every loose ball."

The next five minutes were some of the longest in Aiden's life. The Wolfpack pressed forward but couldn't break through the Thunder defense. Anytime Aiden got the chance, he booted the ball downfield as far as he could.

"Come on, clock," he whispered under his breath. "Get moving."

After what seemed like forever, the referee blew his whistle and crossed his hands over his head.

The game was over. The Thunder had

squeezed out a win and three important points in the standings. They were in first place with just one game to go.

Ava stood on the sidelines, already dressed in her uniform for her game later that afternoon. "Great job!" she called out as Aiden and Daniel walked off the field. "One more win and you guys are on the trophy too!"

Daniel smiled and wiped the sweat from his forehead. "Hey, speaking of the trophy, what's our next move to solve the soccer trophy mystery?"

Aiden almost had to shake his head to rearrange his brain. He was still thinking of the Thunder's narrow win and their one-point lead in the league standings.

"I guess we have to find those newspaper articles," he said finally. "Maybe they'll tell us something new about the case."

CHAPTER
EIGHT

Aiden, Ava, and Daniel raced up the stairs.

"Do you think we'll find anything?" Daniel asked.

"My mom always says you should start any research project at the library," Aiden said as he swung open the door.

"That's probably because her mom worked in one," Ava said.

The three friends quieted down the moment they entered the hushed silence of the building.

"There's Mrs. Salvadore," Ava whispered. "Let's go ask her."

They walked up to the information desk. Mrs. Salvadore peered over her reading glasses.

"Back already?" she asked in a soft tone. "How's it going with *The Age of Innocence*?"

"Uh...fine," Aiden said. "But today we're looking for some old newspaper articles—"

"The *Reporter*," Ava added before he could finish.

Mrs. Salvadore smiled. "You've come to the right place."

She stepped out from the desk and walked across the big room to a corner with some desks and chairs and three metal file cabinets.

"We have every single issue of the town newspaper—the *Reporter*—since 1877," she declared proudly.

Aiden looked around the room. He saw some papers on shelves along one wall, but no big stacks of newspapers.

"Where?" he asked.

Mrs. Salvadore tapped the file cabinets. "Right here. We don't have them digitized yet. They're all on microfilm."

"Micro-what?" Daniel asked.

"Microfilm," she repeated as she opened a drawer of one of the cabinets. "Do you know the year you're looking for?"

"About forty years ago," Aiden said.

Mrs. Salvadore looked at all three friends but didn't say anything. She took out two small, yellowed boxes from the drawer. "I think these should have the year you're looking for."

Then Mrs. Salvadore opened one of the boxes and pulled out a gray plastic spool with what appeared to be some kind of film wound around it. She walked over to a machine that looked a little like an old-fashioned movie projector. She clipped the plastic spool onto the machine and then threaded the film through a glass plate and onto another spool.

The librarian flipped a switch and a screen on the machine lit up. Aiden, Ava, and Daniel crowded around the screen.

"This button makes the microfilm move forward," Mrs. Salvadore explained as the machine whirred and images flashed by the screen. "When you want to stop, push it again so you can see the image."

The machine clicked and sure enough, an image of the front page of an old *Reporter* appeared on the screen.

Mrs. Salvadore pointed to a plastic handle on the side of the machine. "You can use the crank," she explained, "if you want to scroll through the papers more slowly."

She looked back and saw a line of people waiting at the information desk. "You should be all set. If you have any questions, just come and find me. I'll probably be over there."

"Thanks."

Mrs. Salvadore started to walk away, then turned back to the young detectives. "I think the trophy's disappearance made front-page news in Winchester. So you might start by checking the front page of every issue for that year."

Aiden nodded. "Okay, thanks."

The three friends pulled their chairs up to the machine and got to work scrolling through the front pages of the town's weekly newspaper. But they couldn't help stopping to check out the other pages. They noticed quite a few differences from the town they knew and the town of forty years ago.

"There are a million ads," Ava said, pointing to a page filled with announcements from dozens of stores, shops, and restaurants around the town. "Look at them all."

"Check this out," Daniel said. "Here's a brand-new car—a Mercury Marquis, whatever that is—for five thousand dollars. Now cars cost at least five times that."

"Hey, it looks like you could buy a whole house back then for eighty thousand," Aiden said.

When they came to the sports section, Ava pointed to a picture of a boys' high school basketball game.

She laughed. "Look at those uniforms! They are so dorky."

"The shorts are really short," Aiden said.

"And check out the tall socks," Daniel added.

They scrolled through some more of the sports pages. "Nana was right," Ava observed. "It's all boys' sports. There's nothing about the girls' games. It's like they didn't exist."

After almost half an hour of searching through the old newspapers, they found the front-page headline they were looking for.

Aiden almost jumped out of his chair. They all leaned toward the screen to read the article.

SOCCER TROPHY MISSING FROM LIBRARY

Winchester police said that a trophy honoring the county youth soccer champions was reported missing from Winchester County Public Library on Tuesday.

Joseph Palmer, the officer investigating the case, told the *Reporter* that the police are not sure exactly when the trophy disappeared.

"A librarian noticed on Tuesday afternoon that the trophy was not in its usual place in a bookcase in the main reading room. But it may have disappeared earlier than that."

The investigation uncovered no evidence of a forced break-in. Officer Palmer said all the windows and locks at the library were untouched.

The police have questioned the people who work at the library as well as some frequent patrons but so far are stumped as to who would steal the trophy. When asked by the *Reporter* if there were any suspects, Palmer said, "That's the thing. Who would want a soccer trophy? It's not worth much."

He shook his head. "It's a mystery."

They found a few more articles about the soccer trophy on the microfilm. But none of them provided much information that would help in solving the mystery. There was nothing about additional evidence. No suspects. No reason given for anyone to want to steal a trophy. In two to three weeks the story was no longer in the newspaper.

"Joseph Palmer," Aiden said after they had finished reading the last article. "Didn't we used to have a police chief named Palmer?"

"I'm pretty sure we did," Ava said. "He must be this same guy. I guess he was just a regular officer back then."

"My dad knows him," Daniel said. "He retired a couple years ago. I think he still lives up on Knollwood Road."

"We should go talk to him," Ava said.

Aiden nodded. "It's just like in the books and movies. The detective keeps talking to people until he puts the pieces of the mystery together...like a puzzle."

He shut down the machine and put the boxes back in the cabinet.

"So when are we going to put the puzzle together?" Daniel asked Aiden.

Aiden smiled. "First we have to figure out all the puzzle pieces."

CHAPTER NINE

The house on Knollwood Road looked as if it belonged on a picture postcard. Out front, a white picket fence surrounded a trimmed lawn and a well-tended flower garden. An American flag flew from a flagpole in the side yard, flapping in the cool November breeze.

Aiden rang the doorbell. An older man came to the door. He was fit-looking and sported a buzz cut and a neat gray moustache. He looked as if he should still be in a police uniform.

"We're...um...looking for Mr. Palmer," Aiden started. "I mean, *Chief* Palmer..." Aiden could feel his voice wavering. Being a detective was not as easy as it seemed in books and movies.

"Mr. Palmer is fine. I haven't been the chief of police for a couple of years."

Ava took over. "We'd like to talk to you about an old case of yours," she said. "It's for a school project...sort of a town history project."

"Okay. Come on in." Mr. Palmer turned and entered the house. Aiden, Ava, and Daniel followed. The living room was small. A sofa and two chairs faced a brick fireplace. A copy of the *Reporter* was on a coffee table in front of the sofa.

"Would you like to sit down?"

The three teenagers sat side by side on the sofa. A small white dog scrambled into the living room, wagging its tail. It trotted over and put its paws on the arm of the sofa.

"Here, Chips!" Mr. Palmer called. "Don't mind him. He won't bother you." He smiled. "Well, maybe he'd try to lick you to death." The dog walked across the room and settled on the rug a few feet away from Mr. Palmer.

"What case are you interested in?" the policeman asked as he gave the dog's head a pat.

"Do you remember when the county soccer trophy disappeared from the library?" Aiden asked.

Mr. Palmer nodded. "Oh sure," he said and then chuckled. "It's funny how you always remember the cases you *didn't* solve."

"What do you remember about it?" Daniel asked.

Mr. Palmer put his fingertips together and began to tell them the story. "There had been a bunch of B and Es that month around town, but this one was different." He noticed the puzzled look on the kids' faces. "Sorry. B and Es are breaking and enterings. But this was a funny case. It wasn't a break-in. I remember being sure of that. We checked all the doors and windows and none of them had been damaged."

"So whoever took the trophy must have either had a key or was already inside the library?" Ava asked.

"That's right," Mr. Palmer said. "But we doubted anyone would have taken it during library hours. It was a good-sized trophy.

Someone would certainly have noticed a person carrying it out."

"How big was it?" Ava asked.

"They said it was two or three feet tall," Mr. Palmer answered, placing his right palm about a yard above the floor. "I could see how some kid might have wanted it. But as far as we could determine, only a few people had keys to the library. And they were people who worked there."

"Our grandmother—Mrs. Romano—was one of the librarians then," Aiden said. "She says you thought *she* took the trophy."

"We didn't really think she took it," Mr. Palmer said with a chuckle. "You say she's your grandmother? She seemed like such a nice lady. But if I remember correctly, she had a key for locking up the library on the nights she worked late. So naturally we had to ask her some questions."

Mr. Palmer smiled and shook his head. "I mean, what would she want with a soccer trophy?"

"Was that the only thing missing?" Aiden asked. "What about any other trophies?"

"No, nothing else was even moved out of place. That's probably why no one noticed that it was missing at first."

"When did the robbery take place?" Ava asked.

"That's another thing," Mr. Palmer said. "We never determined exactly when the trophy was stolen. It wasn't like someone was checking on it every day. Someone noticed it was gone on Tuesday morning, I think, but it could have disappeared Monday, or even over the weekend. Who knows? Nobody at the library could remember precisely when they had last seen the trophy."

Mr. Palmer leaned forward in his chair. "But that wasn't the biggest problem with the case," he said.

"What was the big problem?" Ava asked.

"You see, whenever you're trying to solve a crime," Mr. Palmer said, eyeing the three friends, "you not only look for people who had the opportunity to commit the crime. You also have to find someone with a motive."

"Motive?" Daniel interrupted.

"Yeah. You know, a reason," Mr. Palmer explained. "Some people, like your grandmother, had the opportunity to get into the library after hours, but they didn't have a motive to steal the trophy."

He leaned back in his chair. "That was the big problem with the case. We never figured out why anyone would want to steal a kids' soccer trophy."

"Were there any other suspects?" Aiden asked.

"Not really," Mr. Palmer said. "Although I always thought Charlie Langston might have taken it."

"Who's he?" Daniel asked.

"He was a soccer coach at the time. Charlie's not a bad guy, but he's a bit of a sore loser. His teams never got on the trophy, so I thought maybe he took it. Or maybe a player from his team."

Aiden looked at Ava and Daniel. That had been one of his theories about who took the trophy.

"But while Charlie may have had a motive to take the trophy," Mr. Palmer said,

65

leaning forward and pointing at the young detectives on his sofa, "he didn't seem to have an opportunity to take it. No one had ever seen him at the library. I don't think Charlie was much of a reader. And as far as we could tell, none of his family had any connection to the library either."

Mr. Palmer shook his head. He seemed like he was still frustrated by the case. "Motive and opportunity," he said. "We never could match those up in that case."

He put his hands on his knees as if he was ready to get up. "Any other questions?" he asked.

Aiden looked at Ava and Daniel. They shook their heads. "I guess that's it," Aiden said. "Thanks a lot."

Mr. Palmer stood up. Chips stood up too, wagging his tail. "If you ever find that trophy or solve the mystery about who took it, you be sure to tell me."

"We will," Aiden said as they moved toward the door. But somehow after talking to Chief Palmer, he doubted they would ever figure out who stole the soccer trophy.

CHAPTER TEN

G ame night," Ava announced after the table was clear and all the dishes were in the dishwater. The twins' school had a policy of no homework on Wednesdays, so the Connelly family played a board game almost every Wednesday night.

"What should we play?" Aiden asked.

"How about Chronology?" Mom suggested.

"No way, you always win that game because you know so much history," Ava said.

"Why don't we play Clue?" Dad suggested.

"Okay, I'll get the board out," Ava said.

Aiden wandered into the kitchen. He checked the bottom few games on the soccer schedule that was posted under a round magnet on the refrigerator. He had scribbled in the scores of the previous games.

OCTOBER 16	10 a.m.	TIGERS	2-1
OCTOBER 23	1 p.m.	LEMONHEADS	4-0
OCTOBER 30	2 p.m.	AVENGERS	2-2
NOVEMBER 6	3 p.m.	WOLFPACK	1-0
NOVEMBER 13	11 a.m.	DRAGONS	

"What time is your game on Saturday?" his father asked.

"Eleven."

"What about yours, Ava?"

"My game's at two," Ava said. "But Coach said she won't play me the whole game because we're already county champs."

"Way to go!" Aiden said and slapped a high five with his twin sister.

"You may be on the trophy too," Ava said. "After Saturday."

Aiden and Ava set up the detective game of Clue on the dining room table and everyone picked a token. Aiden was Colonel Mustard. Ava was Miss Scarlett. Their parents were Professor Plum and Mrs. Peacock.

Without looking at the cards, Dad slipped the three that were the solution to the mystery—the murderer, the weapon, and the room where the crime occurred—facedown into a secret envelope in the middle of the board, then he shuffled the three stacks and dealt the rest of the cards.

It took a while for the game to get going, but after about fifteen minutes they'd moved through several rounds of trying to figure out the solution to the crime.

"Speaking of the trophy," Dad said as he rolled the die and moved his purple token ahead five spaces. "Have you two found any good leads on the mystery of what happened to the old one?"

"Not really," Ava said as she rolled and moved her red token into the conservatory.

"We talked to Nana," Ava said. "She didn't give us much information, but she remembered that the robbery was in the newspapers." Ava checked her Clue sheet and then made her suggestion. "I say it was done in the conservatory with the lead pipe by Mr. Green, and I'm asking Aiden."

Aiden reached under the table and showed her the lead pipe card without showing his parents. Ava marked her Clue sheet.

"And we found the newspapers from the time the trophy disappeared," Aiden said, picking up on his sister's story.

"Where'd you find the *Reporter* from forty years ago?" their mother asked. "Online?"

"No. We found them at the library," Ava said. "Remember, you always told us to begin any research project at the library."

"I guess I did. That's what Nana always said to me."

"They have every issue of the *Reporter* all the way back to 1877," Aiden said. "On microfilm."

It was Aiden's turn to guess. "I say it was done in the billiard room with the rope by Miss Scarlett, and I'm asking Dad." His father showed him the billiard room card.

"So we looked at the original article," Aiden explained after he marked his sheet. "And we found out that a detective named Palmer investigated the case."

"The same Palmer who was the police chief?" Mom asked.

"Yeah," said Aiden. "That's the one."

"He would have been pretty young back then," Dad said. "I think he retired several years ago."

"He did, but we found him," Ava said. "We went to talk to him."

"Is he still in town?" Mom asked. "I haven't seen him around for a while."

"He lives up on Knollwood Road," Aiden said.

"He was police chief here for about twenty-five years." Dad chuckled to himself. "He must know every secret in a town like this."

"Well, he doesn't know who took the soccer trophy," Ava said.

"So it's still a mystery," Dad declared.

The game of Clue continued with everyone taking turns rolling the die and moving their pieces around to the various rooms on the game board. Slowly each player gathered clues about the possible murderer, weapon, and room.

"But Daniel found out something interesting," Ava said, smiling behind her cards. "There's another soccer trophy missing."

"What do you mean?" Dad asked. "What other soccer trophy?"

"The World Cup!" the twins shouted in one voice.

Dad almost dropped his Clue cards. "The World Cup? You're kidding."

"No, it's true. The original trophy was stolen from a place in Brazil back in 1983," Aiden explained. "And it has never been recovered."

"Is it valuable?" Mom asked.

"I don't think the trophy itself is worth much," Ava said.

"But in some ways it's priceless," Aiden added.

"Yeah, but who would want to take it?" Dad wondered aloud. "They wouldn't be able to sell it. Do the authorities think it could still be around somewhere?"

"I'll bet some rich dude in Brazil has it stashed away in a back room in some big house on a mountaintop," Aiden said.

"Maybe, but why steal it if you're never going to show it to anybody?" Ava asked.

"Hey, you young detectives." Their mother was clearly getting impatient with all the talk about soccer trophies. "How is *The Age of Innocence* going?"

The twins' shoulders slumped. "That book is so boring," Aiden groaned.

"Nothing ever happens," Ava chimed in. "I don't know why Ms. Sanchez couldn't have picked a more interesting book."

"It's a classic," Mom said as she rolled the die. "The book gives you insight into how people lived in New York City a hundred years ago."

"Yeah, now we know New York back then must have been really boring," Aiden said.

Dad moved his piece into the ballroom. He checked his sheet and said, "I think it was done in the ballroom by Mrs. White with the candlestick, and I am asking my lovely wife."

Mom looked at her cards and shook her head. "I don't have anything," she said.

"Then I think I'm ready to make a final guess," Dad said and reached for the three cards in the secret envelope. He leaned away from the table and pulled the secret cards out one at a time. He smiled and laid the cards on the table.

"Ballroom, Mrs. White, candlestick," he said and put his hands in the air in triumph.

"Arrrgh," Aiden groaned. "I had Mrs. White and the candlestick, but I thought it was done in the hall."

Mom pushed back from the table. "All right, it's eight-thirty. You still have time to do some reading."

"It's a no-homework night," Ava protested.

"Then read something that's not for school. Go on, upstairs," Mom said with a wave of her hand. "Dad and I will put away the game."

"So you and I didn't solve the Clue mystery, but what's our next move on the soccer trophy mystery?" Ava asked Aiden as they headed up to their rooms.

"I guess we should go talk to that old soccer coach. Remember, Chief Palmer said he might have had a motive to steal the trophy."

"Yeah, but it didn't sound like he had an opportunity," Ava said. "Chief Palmer told us you have to have both."

Aiden shrugged. "Maybe Chief Palmer missed something."

"Should we call Daniel?" Ava asked.

Aiden shook his head. "We can do this one by ourselves."

Ava paused in her doorway and looked back at Aiden. "Remember, Chief Palmer said that coach was kind of mean."

"He was a kids' soccer coach. He can't be too bad," Aiden said. "Can he?"

CHAPTER ELEVEN

I think that's the one," Ava said, pointing to a small house set back from the road.

"Did you see a number on it?" Aiden asked, looking around.

Ava shook her head. "But that one is number 8 and the one over there is number 12. So this one has got to be number 10."

Aiden opened the fence gate to the yard. Once unhooked, the gate sagged to the side. They approached the house slowly. The lawn needed cutting. Big, overgrown bushes covered most of the front windows. Aiden noticed that the paint on the shutters was chipped and one shutter was missing.

"Lions and tigers and bears, oh my," Ava whispered into Aiden's ear, echoing the famous line from the movie *The Wizard of Oz.*

Aiden didn't laugh. His mouth was dry. "It *is* kind of creepy," he said.

"Totally creepy."

The twins stood at the door. A hand-lettered, yellowed index card covered the doorbell.

DOORBELL BROKEN USE THE KNOCKER

Aiden lifted the large brass knocker and let it fall against the wooden door.

He heard a scratching sound and then a loud bark.

"I'm coming, I'm coming!" a voice called from behind the door.

The man who opened the door was dressed in faded blue jeans and an untucked plaid work shirt. His hair needed combing. Aiden could see a large black dog a few feet behind him.

"I've already bought my cookies for this year's soccer season," the man declared before either Aiden or Ava could open their mouths.

"We're not selling cookies," Ava said.

The dog started barking. *Ruff...ruff...ruff.*

The man swung his hand back toward the dog. "Quiet, Bismarck!" he shouted. "Quiet!"

The bark lowered into a growl.

"Are you Mr. Langston?" Aiden asked over the noise from the dog.

"Yeah, why?"

"Could we talk to you for a few minutes?"

"About what?" Mr. Langston did not seem eager to talk to them.

"A soccer trophy," Aiden started. "The one that used to be in the library—"

"The one that was stolen," Ava added.

The dog edged forward, his teeth bared.

"That was thirty...forty years ago," Mr. Langston said, eyeing Aiden and Ava. "What are you kids up to?"

"We're working on a school project," Ava said.

"For the school newspaper," Aiden added.

Mr. Langston did not seem convinced. "School project...school newspaper? What kind of crazy school assignment is this?

Asking people about something that happened so long ago?"

Bismarck lunged forward and started barking again.

Mr. Langston pushed him away. Aiden and Ava stepped back.

"Who said you should talk to me?"

Aiden could now hear the obvious anger in Mr. Langston's voice. "Well, we thought since you were a coach back then, we... um..."

Mr. Langston leaned into the doorway. "Did Chief Palmer send you over here?"

"Not exactly," Ava started with a tremble in her voice. "But he...he said—"

The words were barely out of her mouth when Mr. Langston started shouting.

"Listen to me! I coached for more than twenty years. I must have coached two... three hundred kids. And this is the thanks I get?" He gripped the door tighter. "The refs were always against me...every game. Never gave my teams a break. Not one. What would I want that stupid trophy for anyway?"

Ruff! Ruff! Bismarck was getting more excited listening to his master's shouts.

"We just thought...," Aiden said, daring another attempt to ask Mr. Langston a question, "that you could tell us—"

Mr. Langston pointed a stern finger at the twins. "Get out of here!" He was yelling full force now. "And tell that useless cop Palmer if he ever sends anyone else to my house again...I'll sue him. That's what I'll do...sue him!"

Bismarck leaped at the door, but Mr. Langston caught him by the collar and jerked it back, sending the dog skidding across the wooden floor.

He slammed the door shut so hard, the brass knocker bounced up and banged twice against the wood.

Aiden and Ava walked away from the house quickly. They could still hear Bismarck barking from inside the house. They broke into a run and were halfway down the street when the noise finally faded away.

"Do you think he stole the trophy?" Ava asked, almost out of breath.

"I don't know," Aiden said, finally slowing his pace now that they were safely away. "He's sure mean enough to steal it. But I'll tell you one thing, I'm not going back to find out."

They didn't say much on the way home, but when they reached their driveway, Ava tapped her brother's shoulder with the back of her hand. "Daniel wanted us to tell him how the interview went. Why don't we text him?"

Aiden nodded, took out his phone, and started tapping away.

Talk w/ Langston a dead end.

Daniel answered almost instantly.

OK. Forget the mystery—let's win Sat.

Aiden put his phone back in his pocket. Daniel was right. Maybe they should forget about the soccer trophy mystery and concentrate on beating the Dragons.

Chapter TWELVE

Aiden flopped onto the sideline grass. "How can our team be down 1–0?" he moaned. "We must have missed a million chances to score."

"Yeah," Daniel agreed. "There's no way we should be behind at halftime."

Coach Schmidt clapped his hands to get the team's full attention. "We played well in the first half," he said, trying to pick up the Thunder's spirits. "We just didn't cash in on our scoring opportunities. Twenty-five more minutes to play. Keep the pressure on. We'll start clicking."

The team walked back onto the field for the start of the second half.

"Come on," Daniel said. "We just need one goal."

"We need two," Aiden corrected him. "Remember, we have to *win* this game. No way the Fury is going to lose to or tie the Lemonheads. And a tie for us today won't be enough to get us on the trophy if the Fury win."

The second half started a lot like the first half. The Thunder put pressure on the Dragons goal but couldn't break through.

A centering pass found Aiden open at the top of the penalty area. He wasted no time and drilled a high, hard shot that just whistled over the crossbar. He smacked his palm against his thigh as he hustled back down the field. Another chance at scoring had passed by.

The action stayed stubbornly in the middle of the field. Aiden could feel the minutes and the Thunder's chance at the championship—and their place on the trophy—slipping away.

Alex, the Thunder goalkeeper, gathered

in a weak shot and boomed a kick down-field. A Dragon defender went up to head the ball. He mistimed his jump, however, and the ball skidded off the back of his head and bounced into the Dragons half of the field.

Aiden raced by the defender and with one touch controlled the ball. He looked upfield and saw that the defense was disorganized. The Dragons keeper was shouting and pointing at his defenders.

Now's our chance, Aiden thought as he cut into the middle to put more pressure on the Dragons' scrambling defense. When a defender came up to challenge him, Aiden slipped the ball to Daniel, who was charging into the penalty area.

With a quick flick of his left foot, Daniel set up a booming shot with his right. The Dragons keeper didn't have a chance. The ball flew straight into the net.

Goal! The game was tied 1–1.

"We still need another one!" Aiden shouted as the Thunder celebrated near the Dragons goal. "We have to get one more!"

The goal seemed to give the Thunder a burst of energy. Soon they were beating the Dragons to every loose ball and buzzing around the Dragons keeper, looking for a go-ahead goal.

A low shot skipped toward the far post. The Dragons keeper stretched out along the ground, pushing the ball away from the goal and over the end line just in time.

Corner kick!

Aiden rushed over to the left end line flag. He set down the ball for the kick and looked up.

The Dragons goalkeeper was frantically waving his defenders into position as the Thunder forwards darted around. Aiden bent a low, hard kick into the confusion in front of the Dragons goal. Somehow the ball threaded its way, untouched, through the tangle of legs and bounced off the far post.

For the longest moment, the ball lay still just a few feet from the Dragons goal. Ian McManus, a Thunder forward, took a quick step forward and drilled a shot into the wide-open net.

Goal! Now the Thunder led 2–1.

"How much time is left?" Aiden shouted to the sidelines after the Thunder celebration in front of the Dragons goal let up. Coach Schmidt held up three fingers.

The Thunder's second goal seemed to take all the life out of the Dragons. They played the last minutes as if in a daze. The Thunder beat them to every ball and added an insurance goal in the final minute.

The Thunder had won 3–1! They were the champions of the county's U-14 league. Aiden stood in the middle of the field surrounded by Daniel, Jayden, Alex, Ian, and the rest of his Thunder teammates shouting at the sky.

There was a flurry of hugs, high fives, and pictures being taken by parents.

Arms around each other's shoulders, Aiden and Daniel walked to the sideline where Aiden's mom, dad, and sister waited with raised fists and wide smiles.

There were more hugs, high fives, and pictures. But during a quiet moment, Ava leaned in close to her brother. "You guys did it," she said. "I'm glad you're on the trophy too."

Aiden looked around at the Soccerplex. Scattered patches of orange, red, and yellow leaves still clinging to the surrounding trees stood out against the gray autumn skies. He thought back on each of the day's three goals.

"Yeah, we made it onto this trophy," he said to his sister with a tired smile. "But you know, I still wonder what happened to that first one."

CHAPTER
THIRTEEN

"Why are we going to the library again?" Ava griped. "The weather is beautiful. We should be doing something outside."

The twins were riding their bikes down Pleasant Street in the bright sunshine a few days after the Thunder's big win over the Dragons.

"I just want to check the old newspapers again," Aiden said. "I have this feeling that we missed something."

"Where's Daniel?" Ava asked, pedaling hard to keep up with her brother.

"Playing touch football with a bunch of kids at Forest River Park," Aiden said.

"Which is what we should be doing," Ava muttered.

When they reached the library, they parked their bikes outside and hustled up the stairs.

Mrs. Salvadore smiled as they approached her desk. "You're back. Still working on the case of the missing soccer trophy?"

"We're going to look at the old *Reporter*s again," Aiden explained.

"They're still in the same place," Mrs. Salvadore said, sweeping her hand toward the corner of the big room. "You know the way."

A minute later, Ava handed Aiden the same yellow box as before, and Aiden threaded the microfilm into the machine. He found the original article about the stolen trophy and they both reread it.

"When Chief Palmer says here that he can't understand why anyone would steal a soccer trophy," Ava said, pointing at the screen, "he's saying he doesn't have a suspect with a motive."

"Neither do we," Aiden said. "Let's keep looking in the issues after the trophy disappeared. Maybe we can find something." He scrolled ahead a few pages.

"Hey, look at this," Ava said in an excited voice. "*The Empire Strikes Back* was playing at the Warwick. Man, that movie is ancient."

Aiden went through week after week of the *Reporter*. After the first article on the missing trophy, there were a couple of shorter articles that mostly repeated what Aiden and Ava already knew. Then weeks of nothing—no news on the missing soccer trophy. The trail seemed to go cold.

Aiden was about to give up when Ava almost popped out of her seat. "Wait," she said. "Scroll back to the lower corner of page five."

Then Aiden saw what had caught his sister's eye.

SOCCER LEAGUE TO REPLACE MISSING TROPHY

Christopher Lewis Barron, President of the Winchester County Youth Soccer League (WCYSL), announced this week that the WCYSL will replace the U-14 champions' trophy.

The trophy disappeared from the Winchester County Library in September. Police investigated the incident but have been unable to determine what happened to the trophy.

"We had hoped the trophy would have been recovered or returned by now," Barron told the *Reporter*. "But since it appears that the trophy is gone for good, the board voted to replace it." Barron added that the names of the previous championship teams would be engraved on the new trophy.

In addition, the board voted to purchase another trophy for the U-14 girls' champions. "Girls' participation in the sport is growing," Barron said. "The board felt it was time for the girls to have a trophy too."

Both of the trophies will be displayed in a glass case on the first floor of the library.

"Wait a second," Ava said after finishing the article. "There was one trophy, then that trophy disappears...and now there are two?"

"So what?" Aiden asked, pushing back from the machine.

Ava leaned in closer. "Don't you see? Forty years ago the only trophy was for the boys' championship teams. The girls had been playing for years, but there was no trophy for them."

"I just figured they put the boys' champions and the girls' champions on the same trophy," Aiden said.

Ava reread the last quote from the WCYSL president and shook her head. "It sure doesn't sound like the girls were on any trophy."

Aiden sat for a moment, thinking. But Ava was already ahead of him.

"Remember," she whispered. "Nana said she had a key to the library."

"And Chief Palmer said none of the doors or windows were broken," Aiden added. "So it had to be someone who was already in the library or someone who could get inside the building."

"Now we know there was only one trophy...a boys' trophy," Ava said, her voice getting louder. "Nothing for the girls."

"Yeah, the old newspapers didn't have anything about girls' sports either," Aiden said.

"And remember, both Nana and Mom said nobody cared about girls' sports," Ava said. "Even though Mom was a big star."

Aiden and Ava sat stone-still for several minutes in the silence of the library. Aiden turned the different puzzle pieces of the soccer trophy mystery over in his mind.

The key. The newspaper articles. How no one paid any attention to girls' sports forty years ago. The boys' trophy. And now the new girls' trophy.

It felt as though the pieces of the mystery might be dropping into place. Just like in the books Aiden loved to read and the television shows he watched.

Aiden looked straight at his sister. "Are you thinking what I'm thinking?"

Ava nodded. "I think we may have our motive...let's go!"

Motive and opportunity. Now, like Chief Palmer had said, it was all there. But no one had been able to see it forty years ago.

They put the microfilm away and waved a quick goodbye to Mrs. Salvadore. Once they were out the door, they flew down the steps and hopped onto their bikes.

"Didn't Mom and Dad bring some boxes to our house a couple of years ago when they moved Nana to the Devereaux House?" Ava asked as they started to pedal away.

"Yeah, a bunch of them," Aiden said. "When did Mom say she was coming home?"

"Around five o'clock."

"What time is it now?"

"Four thirty-seven."

"We'd better step on it."

They sped down Pleasant Street, pumping furiously. They hardly noticed the shops or the rows of well-kept houses.

Aiden was in the lead. He had to swerve out of the way when the door of a parked car swung open without warning.

"Whoa, that was close!" Ava called from behind. "You okay?"

"Yeah, keep going!" Aiden shouted, his head down. "We don't have much time."

They turned onto their street, skidded to a stop in front of their house, and ran up the stairs.

It was a quarter of five and they could feel the clock ticking.

CHAPTER
FOURTEEN

The house was quiet when Aiden and Ava burst through the door.

"Mom? Dad?" Aiden shouted. "Anybody home?"

More quiet. Ava stepped into the kitchen and found a note on the counter.

Dad and I will be home around 5 p.m. Having spaghetti. Please take hamburger out of freezer and set table.

Love, Mom

Aiden and Ava ignored all thoughts of dinner and their mother's note for the moment.

"Where do you think all those boxes could be?" Aiden asked.

"The basement?"

Aiden shook his head. "No way. We're down there all the time. We would have seen them."

"How about the attic?" Ava said. "We never go up there."

"We'd better hurry. We only have ten minutes before Mom and Dad come home."

They bolted up the stairs. At the top they turned right and moved quickly down a hallway. Aiden reached up and grabbed the small rope dangling from the ceiling. A door in the ceiling edged down, revealing a folded metal ladder. Aiden pulled the ladder down until the bottom rung rested on the hall floor.

"Remember when we had that bat flying around in the attic?" Ava said as Aiden stepped onto the ladder. "And how awful it smelled? Dad had to call the animal services people...and they came and—"

"Will you stop talking about that bat!" Aiden shouted. He could tell by the way his sister was going on and on about the bat that she was nervous. The truth was, so was he. But it didn't have anything to do with bats. He was wondering what he might find—or not find—in their family attic. Aiden's heart was pounding, and his hands were so sweaty he thought they might slip off the ladder.

At the top of the ladder, Aiden reached up and pulled the string hanging overhead. A single light bulb lit the attic. He scooted around some old backpacks and stepped into the attic. Ava followed right behind him.

The cramped room with the sharply angled ceiling was filled with luggage, boxes of books, and all sorts of other things. Ava saw the trunk that held her old American Girl dolls. Leaning against it were a couple of paintings that had hung in the family living room until Mom declared one day she was tired of looking at them.

"Watch out!" Ava screamed.

"What...*what?*" Aiden shouted, ducking in case it was a flying bat.

Ava pointed to the floor. "You almost stepped on that mousetrap," she said. "Remember when we had those mice up here a few months ago?"

Aiden nudged the trap with his sneaker. *Snap!*

The trap flew into the air and settled on the floor, harmless.

The twins began to open a few boxes but only uncovered old books and photographs. One box was filled with letters written on wafer-thin paper.

"Those are the letters Dad wrote to Mom when she was in the Peace Corps," Ava said. "She said he wrote her almost every day."

"Looks like he did," Aiden said, holding up a handful of letters.

They moved around the attic, opening boxes and checking the other junk that filled the cramped space.

"What's that stuff over there with the tarp on it?" Ava asked, pointing to some boxes tucked into the far corner of the attic.

"I don't remember those from the last time we were up here."

Aiden had to crawl on his hands and knees to reach the pile Ava had discovered. He lifted up the tarp. Several cardboard cartons and one large wooden box were stacked underneath.

"How big did they say the trophy was?" Aiden asked.

"About two or three feet high," Ava answered.

He pulled the wooden box out of the dark corner and pushed it toward the middle of the room, stirring up clouds of dust.

"Aargh!" Aiden screamed and pulled his hand away from the box.

"What happened?" Ava asked.

"I got a splinter," Aiden said, shaking his finger.

Ava ignored him. She was looking for something to pry open the lid. She found an old fireplace poker, stuck it under the lid, and forced the box open. Inside were layers of wadded-up, yellowed newspapers.

"Check it out," Aiden said, still shaking

his finger. "They look like the newspapers we saw on the microfilm at the library."

Sure enough, the papers in the box were from almost forty years ago. Ava and Aiden started to pull them out, scattering the disintegrating fragments on the attic floor.

"Look!" Ava said in an excited voice.

Among the remaining papers was a glint of gold. Aiden and Ava pushed aside more of the packing.

It was a golden soccer player on top of a tall wooden base with gold engraved plates.

Aiden stared at the trophy in amazement. "Holy—"

"Watch your language, young man," a voice called from the entrance to the attic.

Aiden and Ava turned and saw their mother standing on the ladder with only her head and shoulders above the attic floor.

"So you found it," she said.

CHAPTER FIFTEEN

A iden, Ava, and their mother sat in a small circle of chairs in their living room, staring at the trophy on the coffee table. Their father stood a few feet away, behind Ava's chair.

Aiden read the inscription and list of team names on the trophy for the third time.

CHAMPIONS OF THE WCYSL U-14 LEAGUE

United Red
Tigers
United Red
Gunners
Gunners
Wolfpack
United Blue

Aiden looked over at his mother. She was leaning forward, not looking anyone in the eye. Finally she leaned back and broke the silence.

"They used to have a youth football league trophy in the library too." Her voice sounded far away, as if she was back in the time when she was a young girl. "And a Little League trophy. Everything was for the boys. They didn't even let girls play Little League in the county back then."

She shook her head slightly and kept talking, as if she somehow wanted to explain why she had taken the trophy. "Nana and I asked one of the soccer league board members if the girls could have a trophy too. He said the board would look into it, but they didn't do anything. I guess they thought girls sports weren't important enough."

"So Nana knew all along?" Aiden asked.

"She had the key, remember?" Mom took a deep breath. "We took it late one Saturday night after everyone had left the library. Nana and I were just going to hide it away for a while, as a protest against the girls not having a trophy."

"So you and Nana were going to give it back?" Ava asked. Aiden could hear the hope in her voice.

Mom rubbed her lips and chin. "I don't remember exactly what we were thinking. We were just so angry and frustrated that no one was listening to us. We never dreamed it would be such a big deal with the police and everything. And it probably wouldn't have drawn so much attention if it hadn't been for those other break-ins."

"Nana lied to the police?" Ava looked as if she was struggling with the idea that her grandmother and mother had been liars... and *thieves*.

"After it became such a big deal, Nana decided it would be best just to stay quiet about it. She didn't want me to get in trouble." Mom looked away again, staring out the window. "The police never could figure why anyone would steal a kids soccer trophy."

"That's what we couldn't figure out either," Aiden said.

"*We?*" Ava sat straight up in her chair. "I figured it out. Before you."

"That's because you're a girl," Mom said. "Back then people thought the girls didn't mind not having a trophy. I guess they couldn't believe their daughters wanted some recognition too. It was like our sports didn't count."

"It was a different time," Dad said gently.

Mom looked at Dad. "That still doesn't make it right."

"That's true," Dad said, pointing at the trophy. "But speaking of making it right, what are we going to do now?"

Mom leaned back. "At first Nana and I thought about returning it to the cabinet, but we were afraid we might get caught. We could have gotten rid of the trophy after the new trophies were in place, but we were worried someone would find it and start asking questions again."

"We could leave it in the attic," Aiden suggested. "I mean...you know...I don't think it's great you took it but...it's been gone for forty years, and anyway, they have new trophies now."

"Including one for the girls," Ava said

as she traded a small fist bump with her mother.

"Everybody thinks it's gone," Aiden continued. "Just like the World Cup trophy."

Mom shook her head firmly. "I have felt bad about keeping this secret for all these years. I don't want to keep it anymore."

She looked at her two children. "Sometimes I think that's why I encouraged you to work on your soccer trophy mystery. Maybe I wanted you to find out."

"I never thought you guys would figure it out," Dad said. "I figured you would get discouraged and give up. After all, it's been a mystery in this town for forty years."

"You two were a lot better detectives than we thought you would be," Mom said with a small smile. "But now that you know, I don't want you to have to keep the secret too."

"I don't mind," Aiden chimed in. "I mean...I can keep a secret."

"I can keep a secret too," Ava said.

Mom shook her head again. Everyone sat for several silent minutes, thinking.

"Maybe we could give it back to the library," Dad said with a laugh. "Does Nana still have her key to the library? We could sneak in late one Saturday night and put it back."

Mom didn't seem amused at Dad's suggestion. "What would they do with it?" she asked. "They have lots of trophies. They don't need another one."

Aiden fidgeted in his chair. He didn't like the idea of his mother and grandmother stealing anything...even if it was to protest something unfair. He just wanted the problem to go away. "Why do we have to do anything?" he said finally. "I mean, nobody cares about this old trophy anymore."

"Wait a second." Ava stood up suddenly as if she had just remembered something important. "I know one person who cares."

CHAPTER
SIXTEEN

W hat beautiful blue asters."
Chief Palmer, who was on his knees
working in his garden, turned his
head toward Mom.

"Thank you," he said. "I like how they go
with the goldenrod." He pointed his trowel
at a spray of yellow flowers. "The goldenrod is my favorite. This kind is sometimes
called 'Fireworks.'"

Chief Palmer finally noticed Aiden and
Ava. "Oh, it's you two again," he said as he
got to his feet and removed his gardening
gloves. "Mrs. Romano's grandkids, right?
Still working on the case of the missing soccer trophy?"

"Not exactly," Aiden said.

"We wanted to—" Ava began.

Mom put her hand on Ava's shoulder and shook her head slightly to signal her daughter to stop talking. "Could we step inside, Chief Palmer?" she asked. "We have something...personal to discuss."

Aiden, Ava, and Mom followed Mr. Palmer into his living room. Chips trotted in, wagging his tail. Dad arrived in few seconds, carrying the wooden box. He placed it gently on the coffee table. Chips sniffed at the box.

"What's this?" Palmer asked.

"It's the reason we came over," Aiden said.

Mom nodded at the twins, and they lifted the cover. They pushed aside the old newspapers, pulled out the trophy, and stood it on the table.

"Well, I'll be," Chief Palmer said, staring wide-eyed at the object he had worked so hard to find so many years ago. "You *did* solve the mystery. Where did you find it?"

"I took it," Mom said, taking a step forward. "My mother helped me. We've kept it hidden ever since."

Palmer studied Mom for a moment. "So why did you steal it?" he asked, trying to understand.

"It isn't easy, but I'll try to explain. I'm sure you remember that back then only the boys' team had a trophy," Mom said. "We didn't think it was fair."

She paused for a moment, looking down at her feet. "We went to the soccer league and asked if the girls could have a trophy but they didn't pay any attention to us. So we thought if we took the boys' trophy it might help convince the county to get one for the girls too."

"I didn't really think of that," Palmer said. "Maybe because I had two sons."

"Nobody thought much about girls sports back then," Mom said. "That was the problem."

Chief Palmer studied the trophy. He slid his fingers across the engraved names of the championship teams. "That was a long time ago," he said softly, as if he was counting up all the years. "I was just starting out in the police department."

He turned to Aiden and Ava. "They have a trophy for both the boys and girls now, don't they?"

"Oh yeah," Ava answered.

"Our teams are going to be on them for this year," Aiden said, pointing back and forth between his sister and himself. "Both the boys' and the girls' trophies."

"That's good," Chief Palmer said and looked at Mom. "Better than the old days."

"But what do you think I should do?" Mom asked. "I could take the trophy back to the library or maybe even to the police station." She paused and looked at Chips lying on the floor. "I feel like I should admit that I took it. But I would like to keep my mother out of it if we could. She's eighty-four."

Chief Palmer nodded. "I don't think we will have to involve your mother."

An idea flashed across Aiden's mind. "I've got it. Maybe you could give it to Chief Palmer and he could take it back. Let him take the credit for solving the mystery."

Chief Palmer smiled and rubbed his chin.

"I don't think so. That would bring up too many questions. Anyway, I'm not so sure we need to do any of that."

He picked up the trophy. "If I had been smart enough to solve this mystery and we had charged you and your mother what do you think would have happened?

"I don't know," Mom answered.

"My guess is that at most...at most...the court would have required you to pay some kind of restitution," the chief said, answering his own question.

"Resti...what?" Aiden said.

"Restitution," Dad repeated. "It means to pay someone back for something you've broken or damaged."

Chief Palmer nodded. "Listen, I don't like that you and your mother lied to the police and I had to spend hours investigating the case, but there was no real harm done...no one got hurt." Then he added with a chuckle, "I assume you and your mother do not have a criminal record."

Mom shook her head. "No, of course not."

"So a judge back then would have ordered

you to pay restitution. How much would a trophy like this have cost forty years ago?"

"Twenty or thirty dollars, I guess," Mom said.

Chief Palmer nodded. "That's probably about right."

"But—" Mom started.

Chief Palmer held up his hand. "Look, maybe you could make a donation to the WCYSL. Sort of a way to pay them back for the cost of the new trophies and all the trouble you caused. They can always use the money."

"We could make a bigger donation than thirty dollars," Dad said quickly.

"That would be nice," Chief Palmer said. "And probably what a judge might have ordered you to do."

"But shouldn't I tell someone that I took the trophy?" Mom asked.

"You told me," Chief Palmer said.

"But I don't want you to have to keep my secret."

"I was chief of police in this town for almost twenty-five years. I've kept a lot of secrets for a lot of years."

"My children would have to keep the secret too," Mom said as she started to pace the floor. "And I don't want them to think it's okay to steal something."

"We know that!" Aiden and Ava said together.

Chief Palmer looked at Aiden and Ava. "How do you kids feel about keeping your mother and grandmother's secret?"

"I'm okay with it," Aiden said. "Anyway, I wouldn't want Mom or Nana to get in any trouble. Especially Nana."

"I feel the same way," Ava said. "After all, they did it to get the girls a trophy and like Chief Palmer said, there was no real harm done."

"We can let it rest as an old town mystery," Aiden said.

Chief Palmer nodded and placed the trophy back in the box. "And people do love mysteries," he said.

CHAPTER
SEVENTEEN

A iden and Ava sat in the large room at the library reading the final pages of *The Age of Innocence*.

Aiden closed his book and slapped it down on the table with a smack. "Finally," he said in a voice too loud for the library. "Done."

"Keep it down," Ava warned. "I still have two more pages to go."

Mrs. Salvadore came over. "Did you notice anything different in the library?" she asked with a small secret smile.

"What do you mean?" Aiden asked.

"The trophies," she said, spreading her arms wide. "They were engraved this weekend."

Ava closed her book and scrambled out of her reading chair.

"Hey, I thought you wanted to finish the book," Aiden said.

"The heck with *The Age of Innocence*," Ava declared. "I want to see the trophies."

Aiden and Ava walked quickly across the library, trying hard not to run. They stood in front of the trophy case. Sure enough, the trophies had the team names of the new champions of the county's U-14 soccer leagues engraved at the bottom of the plaques.

Wolfpack	**Falcons**
Wolfpack	**Blue Wings**
Fury	**Royals**
Vipers	**Blue Wings**
Thunder	**Spirit**

"Looks pretty good," Daniel said, sneaking up behind the twins.

"When did you get here?" Aiden asked.

"A minute ago."

The three friends viewed the trophies in silence for a minute.

Aiden smiled to himself as he remembered the final games against the Wolfpack and Dragons that got the Thunder on the trophy.

Then Daniel spoke up. "You know, it's funny. Sometimes I still wonder what happened to that old trophy."

Aiden and Ava traded a quick look.

"We'll probably never find out," Ava said finally.

"Yeah," Aiden agreed. "It's like the mystery about the World Cup. My guess is nobody will ever find out what happened to that trophy either."

Daniel nodded, then his face brightened. "Hey, did you hear the big news?"

"About what?"

"Ms. Sanchez assigned a new book for the Advanced English class. It's on her web page."

"Already? What is it?"

"It's another classic. It's called *And Then There Were None*."

The looks on Aiden and Ava's faces showed they had never heard of the book and weren't happy with the choice. "Another classic," Aiden said. "I thought you said this was big news."

"It is!" Daniel almost shouted. "It's by Agatha Christie. This classic is a mystery!"

Aiden, Ava, and Daniel traded high fives. The hand slaps echoed in the quiet room. Aiden broke into a wide, satisfied grin.

"All right!" he said. "I love mysteries."

Keep reading for
THE REAL STORY...

THE REAL STORY

THE MYSTERY OF THE WORLD CUP

Daniel did a good job telling the story about the disappearance of the original World Cup trophy. But there is more to the tale.

Abel LaFleur, a French sculptor, designed the original World Cup for the first world championship soccer tournament played in Uruguay in 1930. The trophy featured a statue of Nike, the Greek goddess of victory, made of gold-plated sterling silver.

In 1946, the Fédération Internationale de Football Association (FIFA), the international organization that runs the World Cup tournament, renamed the World Cup the Jules Rimet Trophy in honor of the FIFA official who had the idea for the World Cup tournament.

By that time, the World Cup trophy had already been through a lot. In 1938, the World Cup trophy was in Italy because the Italian team had won the tournament that year. An Italian sports official named Ottorino Barassi, fearing that German Nazis would steal the World Cup, removed it from a bank in Rome and hid it in a shoebox under his bed for the duration of World War II (1939 to 1945). It must have been a good hiding place, because even though Nazi soldiers broke into Barassi's apartment, they did not find the World Cup. We now know that the Nazis did steal many valuable art objects from the countries they invaded during the war.

When England hosted the tournament in 1966, the trophy traveled to London, where it was displayed at Central Hall in Westminster. On March 20, 1966, four months before the tournament, thieves broke into the hall and stole the trophy.

The World Cup was missing for seven days until a dog named Pickles found it wrapped in newspapers in some bushes while he was on his morning walk. To this day, no one knows who took the World Cup or how it ended up in the bushes. But in recognition of his heroics as a doggie detective, the National Football Museum in Manchester, England, has Pickles's collar on display.

Brazil and Italy played in the finals of the 1970 World Cup in Mexico. Both teams had won the Cup twice and, according to the rules, the winner of the match would get to keep the Cup permanently. In his final World Cup match, Pelé, the legendary soccer great, led a dazzling Brazilian squad to a 4–1 win over Italy, scoring one goal and setting up two more.

After Brazil earned the right to keep the Rimet trophy, FIFA had a new trophy made. This second trophy , the FIFA World Cup Trophy, is the one you now see at the World Cup tournament.

Brazil displayed the Rimet trophy at the offices of the Brazilian Football

Confederation. All was well for many years, but late in the evening of December 19, 1983, a group of thieves overpowered the building's night watchman and stole the trophy from its case.

The Brazilian police investigated the crime but never found the trophy. The police claimed that it was most likely melted down to make gold bars.

But remember, the original World Cup was not solid gold, only gold-plated silver. It probably would have been of little value if it had been melted down. In 2012, Pedro Berwanger, the police officer who led the investigation into the disappearance of the Cup, admitted to a journalist, "Nobody really knows what happened to the Cup. I wouldn't sign a document swearing it was melted down."

So, could the original World Cup—the Jules Rimet trophy—still be out there? And if it is, how much is it worth?

Over the years, several replicas of the Rimet trophy have been made. In 2016, a Swiss watchmaking company, Hublot, bought one of the copies for $525,000. That's more than one half of a *million* dollars for a *fake* trophy. Imagine what the real trophy is worth.

That is, if it is still around.

WOMEN'S SPORTS

Nana and Mrs. Connelly were both right when they said that no one made a big deal out of girls' sports back then.

Of course, not many girls played sports several decades ago. In 1972, only 295,000 girls in the United States played sports in high school. Now, according to the National Confederation of State High School Athletics, more than 3.4 million girls play high school sports. That's a lot more girls participating in basketball, lacrosse, track, and many other sports.

Similarly, there were almost no college athletic scholarships for women years ago. Now, according to the National Collegiate Athletic Association (NCAA), more than 216,000 women play college sports, and many of those athletes earned scholarships.

Why the big difference? Congress passed Title IX of the Education Amendments of 1972. Title IX is the law that requires schools that receive money from the federal government to give their female students the same opportunities as those given to their male students. That includes school sports.

Given the chance, girls now play a lot more sports. Sadly, however, that does not mean people are making "a big deal" of women's sports. Studies show that while women make up approximately 40 percent of athletes, they only receive about 4 percent of the coverage on television and in other media.

It is not clear why women's sports do not get more attention. It's a mystery that people—especially sports fans—should try to solve. The women's games in leagues such as the Women's National Basketball Association (WNBA) and in sports such as tennis, golf, softball, and many more, are fun, competitive, and exciting to watch.

ACKNOWLEDGMENTS

The information about the "mystery of the World Cup trophy" came from the following articles:

"What happened to the lost World Cup?" by Simon Kuper, published in *FT Magazine* on January 30, 2015.

"World Cup mystery: what happened to the original Jules Rimet trophy?" by Paul Gadsby, published in *The Guardian* on June 13, 2014.

"Nazis, Thieves and a Dog Named Pickles: The Unsolved Mystery of the First World Cup Trophy," by Keph Senett, published in *Vice* on August 19, 2016.

The information regarding women's sports came from a column I wrote for the *Washington Post* KidsPost page on August 12, 2010. Additional information on the subject came from the following articles:

"Media Coverage and Female Athletes," by Maribel Lopez, published in *Rewire* on August 10, 2016.

"More women are playing sports. Why is no one watching?" by Kendra Nordin Beato, published in the *Christian Science Monitor* on September 9, 2019.

"High School Sports Participation Increases for 29th Consecutive Year," published in the *NFHS News* on September 11, 2018.

ABOUT THE AUTHOR

Fred Bowen was a Little Leaguer who loved to read. Now he is the author of many action-packed books of sports fiction. He has also written a weekly sports column for kids in the *Washington Post* since 2000.

Fred played lots of sports growing up, including soccer at Marblehead High School. For thirteen years, he coached kids' baseball, soccer, and basketball teams. Some of his stories spring directly from his coaching experience and his sports-happy childhood in Marblehead, Massachusetts.

Fred holds a degree in history from the University of Pennsylvania and a law degree from George Washington University. He was a lawyer for many years before retiring to become a full-time children's author. Bowen has been a guest author at schools and conferences across the country, as well as the National Book Festival in Washington, DC, and the Baseball Hall of Fame.

Fred lives in Silver Spring, Maryland, with his wife Peggy Jackson. Their son is head baseball coach at the University of Maryland, Baltimore County, and their daughter is an elementary school teacher in Washington, DC.

For more information check out the author's website at *www.fredbowen.com*.

ABOUT THE COVER ILLUSTRATOR

 Marcelo Baez, an illustrator and comics artist, is creating new cover illustrations for all the titles in the Fred Bowen Sports Story series. Marcelo has worked for Marvel, ESPN Magazine, and Scholastic, just to name a few. He was born in Chile and lives in Australia. *www.instagram.com/marcelodraws*

HEY, SPORTS FANS!

Don't miss these action-packed books in the Fred Bowen Sports Story series!

All titles available in Ebook editions

BASEBALL

DUGOUT RIVALS
978-1-56145-515-7
Last year Jake was one of his team's best players. But this season It looks like a new kid is going to take Jake's place as team leader. Can Jake settle for second-best?

THE GOLDEN GLOVE
978-1-56145-505-8
Without his lucky glove, Jamie doesn't believe in his ability to lead his baseball team to victory. How will he learn that faith in oneself is the most important equipment for any game?

THE KID COACH
978-1-56145-506-5
Scott and his teammates can't find an adult to coach their team, so they must find a leader among themselves.

LUCKY ENOUGH
PB:978-1-56145-958-2
HC: 978-1-56145-957-5
When Trey's good-luck charm helps him make the Ravens travel team, it reinforces his superstitious behavior. For a while his hitting and fielding gets better and better. But one day his lucky charm goes missing and his performance on the team starts to slip. Is his future with the Ravens doomed?

PERFECT GAME
PB: 978-1-56145-625-3
HC: 978-1-56145-701-4
Isaac is determined to pitch a perfect game. He gets close a couple of times, but when things go wrong he can't get his head back in the game. Then Isaac meets an interesting Unified Sports basketball player who shows him a whole new way to think about perfect.

PLAYOFF DREAMS
PB: 978-1-56145-507-2
Brendan is one of the best players in the league, but no matter how hard he tries, he can't make his team win.

T. J.'S SECRET PITCH
PB: 978-1-56145-504-1
T. J.'s pitches just don't pack the power they need to strike out the batters, but the story of 1940s baseball hero Rip Sewell and his legendary eephus pitch may help him find a solution.

THROWING HEAT
PB: 978-1-56145-540-9
HC: 978-1-56145-573-7
Jack throws the fastest pitches around, but lately his blazing fastballs haven't been enough. He's got to learn new pitches to stay ahead of the batters. But can he resist bringing the heat?

WINNERS TAKE ALL
PB: 978-1-56145-512-6
Kyle makes a poor decision to cheat in a big game. Someone discovers the truth and threatens to reveal it. What can Kyle do now?

BASKETBALL

THE FINAL CUT
PB: 978-1-56145-510-2
Four friends realize that they may not all make the team and that the tryouts are a test—not only of their athletic skills, but also of their friendship.

FULL COURT FEVER
PB: 978-1-56145-508-9
The Falcons have the skill but not the height to win their games. Will the full-court zone press be the solution to their problem?

HARDCOURT COMEBACK
PB: 978-1-56145-516-4
Brett blew a key play in an important game. Now he feels like a loser for letting his teammates down—and he keeps making mistakes. How can Brett become a "winner" again?

OFF THE RIM
PB: 978-1-56145-509-6
Hoping to be more than a benchwarmer, Chris learns that defense is just as important as offense.

ON THE LINE
PB: 978-1-56145-511-9
Marcus is the highest scorer and the best rebounder, but he's not so great at free throws–until the school custodian helps him overcome his fear of failure.

OUTSIDE SHOT
PB: 978-1-56145-956-8
HC: 978-1-56145-955-1
Richie Mallon has always known he was a shooter. He practices every day at his driveway hoop, perfecting his technique. Now that he is facing basketball tryouts under a tough new coach, will his amazing shooting talent be enough to keep him on the team?

REAL HOOPS
PB: 978-1-56145-566-9
Hud can run, pass, and shoot at top speed. But he's not much of a team player. Can Ben convince Hud to leave his dazzling–but one-man–style back on the asphalt?

FOOTBALL

DOUBLE REVERSE
PB: 978-1-56145-807-3
HC: 978-1-56145-814-1
Four friends realize that they may not all make the team and that the tryouts are a test–not only of their athletic skills, but also of their friendship.

QUARTERBACK SEASON
PB: 978-1-56145-594-2
Matt expects to be the starting quarterback. But after a few practices watching Devro, a talented seventh grader, he's starting to get nervous. To make matters worse, his English teacher is on his case about a new class assignment: a journal.

SPEED DEMON
PB: 978-1-68263-077-8
HC: 978-1-68263-076-1
Eager to find his place at his elite new school, ninth-grader Tim Beeman is torn between running track and trying out for football. Where will he feel most comfortable and be able to put his fast running skills to best use?

TOUCHDOWN TROUBLE
PB: 978-1-56145-497-6
Thanks to a major play by Sam, the Cowboys beat their archrivals to remain undefeated. But the celebration ends when Sam and his teammates make an unexpected discovery. Is their perfect season in jeopardy?

SOCCER

GO FOR THE GOAL!
PB: 978-1-56145-632-1
Josh and his talented travel league soccer teammates are having trouble coming together as a successful team—until he convinces them to try team-building exercises.

OUT OF BOUNDS
PB: 978-1-56145-894-3
HC: 978-1-56145-845-5
During a game against the Monarchs, Nate has to decide between going for a goal after a player on the rival team gets injured, or kicking the ball out of bounds as an act of good sportsmanship. What is the balance between playing fair and playing your best?

SOCCER TEAM UPSET
PB: 978-1-56145-495-2
Tyler is angry when his team's star player leaves to join an elite travel team. Just as Tyler expected, the Cougars' season goes straight downhill. Can he make a difference before it's too late?

SOCCER TROPHY MYSTERY
PB: ISBN 978-1-68263-179-2
HC: ISBN 978-1-68263-078-5
Soccer-playing twins Aiden and Ava are devoted to the game, and they are both playing hard to lead their teams to a championship season. Still, they find the time to try to unravel the long-standing mystery of their town's missing soccer trophy.